MW01259009

Green Ivy Publishing

1 Lincoln Centre

18W140 Butterfield Road

Suite 1500

Oakbrook Terrace IL 60181-4843

www.greenivybooks.com

ISBN: 978-1-943955-37-4

Sally The Sea Turtle

Gayle Hooks

One day Sally, for some reason, started on a journey she did not really understand herself. She started swimming to a place she didn't remember ever being. She swam and swam, amazed at all the different things she saw that she never knew existed. She knew something was different about her, but she didn't really understand what was happening. Sally was starting on the journey to have her babies at the place where she had been born. You see, turtles return to where they were born to have their babies in almost the exact same place.

Sally swam for miles and miles, and the ocean was so different from where she lived. She was excited to see all the new animals and sea life. She first ran into a shark. He was not very friendly when Sally tried to ask about where he lived and where he was going, so she continued on her way.

The next things she saw were schools of beautiful fish. They all swam quickly around her, and she asked them where they were going in such a hurry. Then she saw a dolphin eat one of the fish. She thought for sure the dolphin would stop and tell her where they were going, but it seemed everyone was in such a hurry to play and eat, so Sally continued on her journey.

The next creatures she saw amazed her because she could see through them. She swam up to one of them and asked, "What are you, and what is your name?"

"My name is Juliet, and I am a jellyfish," the strange-looking creature replied. Sally couldn't help laughing at this sight. There were hundreds of them everywhere.

Sally was so tired, so she decided to rest some. While resting, some fish decided to feed on the tiny creatures that were attached to her shell. She giggled inside as they surrounded her, even going under her belly. They tickled a little and made her smile.

Sally went to the surface to get some fresh air and looked up to see something she thought was so funny. A big, feathery thing fell from the sky and hit the water. She went over to ask, "Are you okay?"

The bird said, "Yes. I am catching my dinner."

Sally said, "What animal are you?"

The feathery animal said, "My name is Parker, and I am a pelican. My beak can hold more than my belly can!"

Sally was having so much fun with this adventure and decided to continue on. She dove to the bottom of the ocean floor and noticed a funny creature with six legs and funny eyes on top of its head. Sally swam over and asked, "Who are you?"

He said, "My name is Cooper, and I am a crab." Then he quickly ran away.

Sally said, "Don't be afraid. I will not hurt you," but the crab was gone in a flash.

Sally continued on her journey. Just a short time later she saw another animal on the ocean floor. It was red and scary with two big pincers. She kept her distance but asked, "Who are you?"

He said, "I am a lobster, and my name is Logan. Why do you ask?"

Sally replied, "I have never seen anything like you before. I was wondering what you eat, and is this where you live?"

The lobster said, "I eat mussels, crabs, clams, and small fish, and this is where I live, as long as the water is calm and warm."

Sally said, "My favorite thing to eat is seaweed because it tastes so good and keeps me healthy." The lobster wasn't interested, so he went on his way.

Sally took off again and swam close to the surface to see where she was and to get some fresh air. She looked around and couldn't see land in any direction, just a fishing boat.

Sally swam for a long time and came across a large black animal. This was the largest animal she'd ever seen. She swam up next to it and said, "Good morning, what type of animal are you?"

The big animal said, "I am a right whale, and my name is Winter. What are you?"

Sally said, "Oh, you are the first to ask me. I am a sea turtle, and my name is Sally." Then Sally asked, "Where are you going?"

Winter the whale said, "I am not sure. I'm just following the rest of the whales. Where are you going?"

Sally said, "I am going back to where I was born." The whale wished her good luck and swam away.

Sally was having so much fun with her adventure. She was looking at all the animals, and she saw a sea horse and a lot of other turtles that seemed to come from different places. Some of the turtles looked like her, but others looked so different. She swam up to one and asked, "What type of turtle are you?"

The huge turtle said, "I am a leatherback turtle, and my name is Layla."

Sally said, "I am a loggerhead, and I am three hundred pounds, but you are so much bigger than me!"

The leatherback said, "Yes, I am the largest of all sea turtles, and I weigh over one thousand three hundred pounds."

Sally was feeling tired but knew her journey was coming to an end. With each day passing she felt like she had learned so much about so many different animals she now called friends. Can you remember the names of her friends?

Sally surfaced to see how close she was to home. She was delighted to see the most beautiful beach she had ever seen. It seemed so familiar that she instantly knew it was the right place. Sally was filled with so much happiness knowing that she was home again.

Sally saw things moving on the beach and waited for darkness to come before going ashore. This was her time to relax and just float in the waves. She felt calm and knew this was where her babies would be born.

Once darkness was upon the beach, Sally started swimming toward the shore. The crashing of the waves and the pull of the current caused Sally to struggle to get to the beach. One big wave and Sally was finally on land again. She was tired but knew just what she needed to do. She used her large flippers to drag herself through the sand. Once she reached the dunes, she knew this was the perfect place. Sally could not see light from anywhere, except for the moon that would show her the way back to the ocean. Here was where she would dig the hole and make the nest to lay her eggs.

After Sally was at the edge of the dune, she started digging as fast as she could. Once she started, she was like a machine, just throwing the sand everywhere and getting the hole ready for her new family. Once the nest was finished, she began laying her eggs.

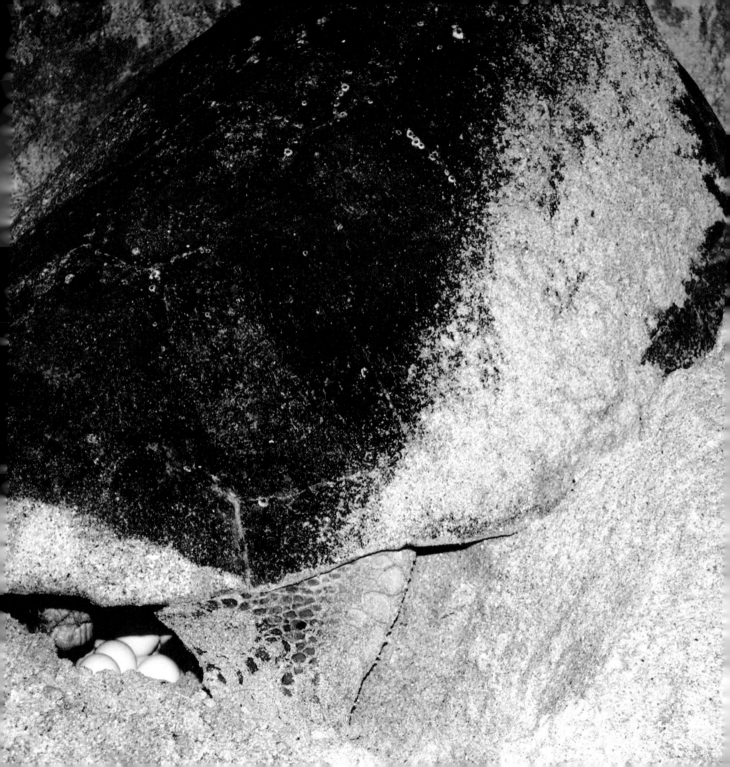

Sally was so tired, but she was filled with so much happiness knowing her babies would begin their lives on the most beautiful beach in the world. After she had all her eggs in the nest, she carefully began to cover them up.

Sally said a prayer to thank the sea for helping her get back to have her babies on the same beach where she had been born. Sally saw her tracks and knew that the tide would erase them again as it once did her mother's.

As Sally finished covering her nest, she saw a human that she knew would not harm her or her babies, so she turned and headed back into the sea to begin her journey back to where she now lived. Sally was happy knowing her babies would start their lives just as she had.

CPSIA information can be obtained
at www.ICGtesting.com
Printed in the USA
LVIC04n0801091015
457524LV00003B/4